TRIPLE TROUBLE
IN HOLLYWOOD

by Michael J. Pellowski

illustrated by Estella Lee Hickman

To A Future Hollywood Star
MORGAN

Published by Willowisp Press, Inc.
401 E. Wilson Bridge Road, Worthington, Ohio 43085

Copyright © 1989 by Willowisp Press, Inc.

Printed in the United States of America

10 9 8 7 6 5 4 3 2

ISBN 0-87406-383-3

One

"HOLLYWOOD!" I said with a sigh, leaning way back in the airplane seat. I closed the romance novel I was reading. "I can't believe we're really going to spend part of summer vacation in Hollywood."

"Uh-huh," my twin sister Randi grunted. She didn't even look up from the fan magazine she had her nose buried in. Randi had bought a whole stack of fan magazines at the airport before we took off for California. Usually, the only thing she ever likes to read is the sports section in the newspaper. Around our house, I, Sandi Daniels, am the bookworm twin. My darling sister Randi gave me that title because I devour romance novels. Sometimes Randi acts like it's a crime to be sentimental. Can I help it if sad stories make me cry? I'm just the emotional type.

I went on. "We'll spend two whole weeks at Aunt Peg and Uncle Nick's. We'll have two fun weeks to spend with Cousin Mandy. And best of all—there will be no Trouble around to bother us!"

Trouble is our name for our little brother Teddy. Randi and I both love Teddy. But he sure can be a pain sometimes. A vacation away from Teddy is like, well, a vacation away from trouble. Teddy and our parents were flying out later to join us for part of our vacation. Until then, it was going to be one big blast.

"It sure will be great to see Mandy again," I said. "I've missed her since she came to visit with us last summer."

"Uh-huh," Randi muttered as she flipped a page.

I looked at my twin sister. For two girls who are supposed to be identical, we sure are different in a lot of ways. To start off, Randi's a sports nut. She's good at anything athletic. And she is absolutely ga-ga over the color red. I'd say 75 percent of all the clothes in her wardrobe are red.

As far as the color red and sports are concerned, I can take them or leave them. Oh, I like playing soccer. Randi and I take turns being the goalie for our local team. But sports is something I could live without if I had to.

Books, music, and the colors pink and purple I could not live without. Like I said, I'm a sucker for a sentimental romance story. Music is my second love. I adore singing. Miss Morgan, one of my teachers, says I have the best voice in the school choir. And I love pink and purple. Almost all of my clothes are one of those two colors. That's why it's always easy to tell Randi's stuff from my stuff.

In fact, it's easier to tell our stuff apart than it is to tell Randi and me apart. We really do look like someone ran one of us through a copying machine. Oh, I'm forgetting all about Cousin

Mandy. You see, Mandy is the same age as us, and she looks exactly like Randi and me. And it's easy to understand why. Uncle Nick is my Dad's older brother, and Aunt Peg is my Mom's younger sister. Two brothers married two sisters. Now if that isn't romantic, what is? It's just like something out of a romance novel.

"I was just thinking about Uncle Nick and Aunt Peg," I said to Randi.

"Uh-huh," she replied as she flipped another page of her fan magazine.

"Is uh-huh all you can say?" I asked. "Aren't you excited about seeing Mandy? We might even get to see her make a commercial at a TV studio!"

"I know! I know! Calm down, Sandi," Randi whispered. "People are looking at us." Randi slumped in her seat and hid her face behind her magazine.

I looked around. Randi was right. I saw the other passengers on the plane shift their eyes away from us. But a bald man and a white-haired lady kept staring at me from across the aisle. Boy, did I ever feel like a nerd! I smiled at them. The lady returned my smile and then went back to her knitting. The bald man just shook his head. I guess he thought I was loony or something.

I leaned close to Randi. "If you'd answer me when I talk to you, people wouldn't look at me like I'm crazy!" I whispered.

"Look, Sandi," she said impatiently. "Just pretend you don't know me." Randi peeked across the aisle at the bald guy. He was still watching us.

"Oh, right," I said. "I'm supposed to just pretend I don't know this identical twin sitting in the seat next to me! Randi, aren't you excited about this trip at all?"

"Sure, I am," Randi replied. "Really. I'm excited. I just don't want to act like a goofy tourist. After all, I do have relatives in show business." She smiled.

"Is that why you keep reading those fan magazines?" I asked.

"Humph!" grunted Randi. "There happens to be something in these magazines I'm interested in," she explained.

"Oh, yeah. What?" I asked.

Randi lowered the magazine and tapped a fingertip on one of the photos inside. "Him," she said in a dreamy sort of way.

I looked down at the picture. It was a photo of a tall, dark-haired teenage boy with pearly white teeth. He had a blue sweater tied around his neck. I had to admit he was kind of cute. He looked familiar, but I couldn't remember where I'd seen him before. "So, who is he?" I asked.

Randi looked at me like I had just arrived from Neptune. "Don't you know?" she asked.

"Is he on a TV show?" I asked.

"He's Judd Morrison," said Randi.

"Oh," I said, shrugging my shoulders.

"I can't believe you," Randi said. "Everybody on this planet knows who Judd Morrison is." She rolled her eyes the way she does at home sometimes when she and Jamie Collins, her best

8

friend, gang up on me.

"He's a semi-regular on *The Reckless and the Ambitious*," Randi explained.

"Oh," I said, "you mean that silly soap opera you always watch?"

"Yes, that soap opera I watch," Randi said in a snippy way. "But any soap opera with Judd Morrison in it is definitely *not* silly!"

"Well," I answered, "I only like the really romantic soaps. The one that you watch is ridiculous."

"What's so ridiculous about it?" Randi demanded.

The bald man across the aisle was looking at us again. I guess our argument was getting a little loud.

"What's so ridiculous about it?" Randi asked again in a softer tone. "I think the show is great. And I think Judd Morrison is a super actor."

I shrugged. "Any show about the president of a big corporation who moonlights as a movie stunt-man is totally ridiculous," I said.

"Well...maybe," Randi admitted. "But Judd's character is totally believable."

"Who does he play?" I asked.

"He is Johnny Leather, the adopted son of a lady motorcycle gang member who is really the lost heir to a vast fortune," explained Randi.

"Now that's totally believable," I said, nodding my head.

"Well, Judd makes the part believable," said Randi. "He's awesome. I'd give anything to meet him." Randi eased back in her seat and sighed. Suddenly, she sat up and asked breathlessly, "Do you think Mandy knows him?"

"I doubt it," I replied. "He looks a lot older than us. Besides, Mandy does commercials, not soaps."

Randi dropped her head back against the seat cushion. I noticed that the bald man was still watching us. I smiled at him once again. This time he smiled back and then shook his head. He whispered something to the lady, and she nodded.

The stewardess stopped by us and smiled. "Fasten your seat belts, girls. We'll be landing shortly," she said. "I hope you had a nice trip."

"Oh, we did," Randi replied. "But the best is yet to come!"

I nodded. Randi and I fastened our seat belts. "Look out, Hollywood," I whispered to my twin sister. "Here come the Daniels Twins!"

Two

ONE of the loneliest feelings in the world is when you get off of an airplane in a strange city. You walk into a crowded airport and don't know a single person.

"Gee, this is kind of scary," Randi said as we walked along looking for Cousin Mandy, Aunt Peg, or Uncle Nick. I nodded. There certainly were some strange-looking folks in that airport. Some of the outfits were so bizarre that it almost made me feel like we'd landed on a different planet. "California fashions aren't like the ones back home," Randi said to me.

"That's for sure," I replied as we headed for the baggage claim area to pick up our luggage.

"Some of these people look like aliens."

When we reached the baggage claim area, we found the bald man from the plane standing there with a suitcase in his hand.

"Good-bye, girls," he said to us. "You certainly made the flight out here very interesting." He chuckled and walked away.

"I guess he was a nice man after all," I said to Randi.

"Here's your suitcase," Randi said. "Mom said to stay away from strangers."

"I was just being polite," I answered as Randi lifted her bag. We turned around, and we both spotted Mandy at the same time. Her blond hair was styled in a really cute way. She had on a short, denim skirt. As usual, Mandy looked great!

"Sandi! Randi!" she shouted and broke into a trot toward us.

"Mandy!" we yelled back. Behind Cousin Mandy came Aunt Peg and Uncle Nick.

"Randi! Sandi! I'm so glad you're here at last!" Mandy squealed as the three of us hugged and

kissed each other hello.

"You both look super," Mandy said as we hugged and kissed some more.

"Hey! Save some of that for us," Uncle Nick said as he and Aunt Peg walked up.

"Hi, Uncle Nick," I said and gave him a great big hug. Randi hugged and kissed Aunt Peg. Then we switched and repeated the whole scene.

"Let me take a look at you three," Uncle Nick said. He stepped back from Randi, Mandy, and me. We put our arms around each other and smiled, like someone was taking our picture.

"The Three Musketeers are reunited," Mandy said.

"It's just amazing," Uncle Nick said to Aunt Peg. "It's easy to see how they switched identities last summer and got into all that trouble."

"It certainly is," Aunt Peg agreed. "It's like looking in a three-way mirror. Randi or Sandi could stand in for Mandy, even in a close-up."

"But there won't be any of that switching stuff out here," Uncle Nick said. He picked up our suitcases and winked at us. "We don't need that kind of trouble in Hollywood."

The three of us giggled. We were all thinking about the time Mandy pretended to be us, and Randi and I got even by both pretending to be her.

"Let's go, everyone," Aunt Peg said. "Tonight I'm going to make a special spaghetti dinner."

"Spaghetti?" teased Randi. "You mean Mandy isn't on a salad diet anymore?"

Mandy laughed and elbowed Randi in the ribs. "Don't worry, Cousin," she said. "I'm not Hollywood star-struck anymore." She pointed at her face. "See, I'm hardly even wearing any makeup." All she had on was a little face blush and a light shade of lipstick. I remembered the first time I'd seen my cousin. She looked like a makeup grenade had exploded in her face.

"That's still more than Mom lets us wear," Randi said as we walked out of the airport terminal with our arms around each other.

"Speaking of being Hollywood star-struck," I

said to Mandy. "What's new in your career? Have you done any commercials lately?"

"It's a long story," sighed Mandy in a way that made me curious. "I'll tell you all about it when we get home. Right now, let's catch up on what's new with you guys. How are Chris Miles, Jamie Collins, and good old Bobbi Joy Boikin?" Mandy asked. Chris and Bobbi Joy are kids Mandy met when she visited us. Jamie is our best friend back home.

"We'll fill you in during the drive," Randi answered.

"I want to hear all about your mom and dad and little Teddy, too," Aunt Peg said as she looked back at us.

"Here's the car," Uncle Nick announced. He unlocked the doors and put our bags in the rear of the station wagon. "We're off," he said as he got in and started the engine.

The three of us chattered and gabbed so much that Randi and I almost forgot to look around at the wonderful world of southern California!

Three

"YOUR room is totally awesome!" Randi exclaimed as she sat on Mandy's bed and looked around. On the walls were autographed pictures of celebrities and lots of movie posters. There were also publicity shots of Mandy posing with some of the products she'd done commercials for. And Mandy's room was huge. Even with the portable beds that Randi and I would be sleeping on, the room seemed gigantic. "This is some big room," Randi continued. "And it's so...clean!"

"Mom likes me to keep my things in order," Mandy said.

"That won't last long," I interjected. I placed

my suitcase on the bed and opened it. "Just give Randi a little time. She'll turn this place into a pigpen just like our room back home." Randi sat up and glared at me. "I'm just kidding, sister dear," I apologized.

Randi patted her stomach. "That was a great snack your mom fixed us," Randi said to Mandy. "It was nice the way we all sat around the table talking about the good old days before you guys moved out here."

Suddenly, Randi burped. "Excuse me," she apologized.

We all laughed. "You wouldn't do that if you didn't always stuff yourself," I said. "You won't have any room for that spaghetti dinner tonight."

"Don't worry. I'll have room," Randi assured me. "An athlete needs her strength," she continued as she plopped back down on Mandy's bed. "And I'm an athlete." Randi turned to Mandy. "Do you want to see me do a flip? I've been taking gymnastic lessons." She sat up and hopped off the bed.

"Really?" Mandy replied.

"I don't think it's a good idea to do flips in the house on a full stomach," I said. "You don't want to you-know-what."

"That's true," Randi agreed. She patted her tummy and sat back down. "But I really can do a good flip. I can walk on my hands, too."

"She really can," I told Mandy.

"I wish I could do a flip," Mandy sighed. "Then I might have a chance of getting this commercial I'm auditioning for the day after tomorrow. It's a callback, and I'm a finalist."

"What kind of commercial is it?" I asked. "You said you were going to tell us about your career when we got here. Well, now we're here."

"Yeah," Randi chimed in. "What's the latest Hollywood gossip about Mandy Daniels?"

Mandy walked over to her vanity table and sat down. "The commercial is for Purple Power Bubble Gum," Mandy replied. "And the gossip about Mandy Daniels is that her career is going right down the tubes."

"Huh?" I exclaimed. "What do you mean?"

"I mean I haven't gotten a commercial in months," Mandy said sadly.

I didn't understand. Mandy really is a good actress. She has a natural way of delivering her lines, and she never misses a cue. And she looks super cute on camera. "What's wrong?" I asked.

"I'm not doing anything wrong," Mandy explained. "I've been a finalist for the last three jobs I auditioned for. I was competing against a girl who goes to my school named Tara Butler."

"Tara Butler," Randi said. "What does she look like?"

"She's cute," Mandy admitted. "She has curly, red hair and freckles. She comes from a show biz family. All the kids at school call her Tinsel Town Tara."

"She sounds like the kid on the Super Pops cereal commercial," I said. "You know, she's the one who says, 'Yum-Yum-Yummy for your tummy, Super Pops!' Super Pops is my little brother's favorite breakfast cereal."

"Yeah, that's her!" Mandy cried.

"I can't stand that commercial," groaned Randi. She made a stupid face. "Yum-Yum-Yummy, Super Pops! YUK!"

"So, the commercials were between you and Tara. What happened?" I asked.

"It's simple. Tara got the jobs," Mandy said.

I really felt bad for Mandy. But things like that happen in show business. One minute you're a star. The next minute you're a has-been. "I guess that's the way it goes," I said.

"What really bugs me," Mandy complained, "is that Tara is good, but not *that* good. Her uncle is an assistant director, and he helps her get a lot of parts."

"Ah-ha!" cried Randi. "It's the old who-you-know, not-what-you-know routine." She shook her head and rolled over on the bed.

"Well," I began, "I've heard that's part of show business. It's part of life, too."

"I know," sighed Mandy. "But that darn Tara is such a snob! She thinks she's the greatest.

24

Every time she beats me out, she really rubs it in. Just once I'd like to teach her a lesson." Mandy sighed again. "But it'll never happen. She'll probably get the Purple Power Bubble Gum job, too."

"She's the other finalist?" I asked as I put my blouses in an empty dresser drawer.

Mandy nodded. "Yeah, and her uncle is part of the shooting crew."

"I hate that Super Pops commercial," Randi said again.

"If I could only do a back flip and sing a little better, at least I'd stand a chance against Tara," Mandy continued.

"What do you mean?" Randi asked.

Mandy explained. "In addition to speaking lines for this commercial, I have to sing a jingle and do a back flip."

I looked at Mandy. "Can Tara do those things?"

"Yeah," replied Mandy. "Her parents hired a gymnastics teacher and a voice coach to help her when they heard about the part. We can't afford stuff like that."

"The kid sounds spoiled to me," Randi said as she got up off the bed.

"She is," Mandy admitted. "With the coaching and her uncle's connections, she's sure to get the part. I'm just not good enough at gymnastics or singing."

"It's not fair," Randi complained as she stormed around the room. "It's as if Mandy has to audition against more than one person."

Suddenly, Randi stopped dead in her tracks. A strange gleam lighted her eyes. A devilish smile spread across her face.

"Uh-oh," I said to Mandy. "I know that look. She's hatching one of her schemes."

"Just suppose," said Randi slowly, "that Mandy was more than one person."

I looked at Mandy. Mandy looked at me.

"No," Mandy said shaking her head.

"Nope! No way! It's out of the question!" I echoed. "We can't do the old switcheroo."

Randi nodded. "Why not?" she asked.

"Because every time we try something like that, we end up in trouble," I reminded my sister.

"Yeah," agreed Mandy. "Don't you remember what happened last summer?"

"It's the perfect way to get back at Tinsel Town Tara," Randi explained. "We all go to the audition dressed the same. Sandi sings the jingle. Mandy says the lines. And I do the back flip. We can't miss, and no one will find out."

"No. It's wrong. It's dishonest. And it'll never work," I said, slamming the dresser drawer.

"It might work," Mandy said.

I looked at my cousin. *Uh-oh,* I thought, *she's got the same strange look Randi has.*

"There's a dressing trailer on the set for people who audition," she continued. "I could sneak you two into the trailer. We could use some excuse like having to go to the bathroom to go off the set between takes. Switching places would be hard, but we could do it."

"No! No! No!" I argued. "Getting a role that

way would be totally wrong."

"Yeah," agreed Randi, "I guess it would be." She shook her head. "I just thought maybe we could teach Tara a lesson."

"What if we did the switch and I got the part," said Mandy, "but I suddenly got sick and couldn't do the final cut for the commercial," Mandy proposed. "Tara would get the part, but only after I beat her out. Then we wouldn't be doing anything wrong."

"Not bad!" shouted Randi. "How about it, Sandi?" They both looked at me. The way they stared at me made me really nervous.

What could I say? How could I say no? I had to help Mandy. She sounded like she was losing confidence in herself. And Tara sounded like such a snob. Besides, I really hated that Super Pops commercial, too. "Oh, why not?" I gave in. "But how will we explain it to your mom?"

"I always go on the set alone," Mandy said. "I'll just tell mom you're going along to watch. It's perfectly natural."

"Then it's all settled!" Randi shouted. "Look out, Tinsel Town Tara! Here comes the Daniels gang!"

We all shook hands. Then Randi said, "There's only one more thing I want to know."

"What?" asked Mandy.

"Are you sure you don't know Judd Morrison?" Randi asked.

"For the 97th time, no!" Mandy shouted.

Randi shrugged her shoulders. "Well, there's no harm in asking," she said. We all laughed.

Four

O N the afternoon of Mandy's audition, I was
still pretty nervous about Randi's plan to
switch places. I was sure something bad was
going to happen. Randi must have read my mind.
While we were driving to the studio for the audition, Randi leaned over to me and whispered,
"Will you stop worrying?"

"I'll try," I whispered back.

"What are you girls whispering about back
there?" Aunt Peg asked from the front seat.

Mandy looked back at us and snickered.
"Don't mind them, Mom," she said as she winked
at us. "You know how twins are. They always
have their little secrets."

"Okay. I won't pry," Aunt Peg replied. "But are you sure you're going to be all right at the audition? You don't mind if I just drop you off and then go grocery shopping, do you?"

"We'll be fine," Mandy told her mom. "Did you clear it with the studio people?"

"I talked to the head of the security department," Aunt Peg explained. "Everything's all arranged."

"Great," Mandy said. "Don't worry, Mom. We really can take care of ourselves. Besides, we need those groceries with two extra mouths around to feed."

"The way Randi eats, it's like three extra mouths," I added.

Mandy chuckled. "Randi wolfed down that spaghetti the other night like she was in a race," she said.

"And she finished by knocking five seconds off her best time at home," I added.

"So, I like spaghetti," Randi said. "Stop picking on me, you guys."

"Yeah, stop picking on Randi," Aunt Peg said and laughed.

"Hey, I thought *I* was the sensitive twin," I said.

"We're only kidding, Randi," Mandy apologized.

"I know," Randi admitted. "But all this talk about food is making me hungry." We all laughed. Even Randi laughed at herself. I was glad everyone was talking and joking. It made me feel less nervous about what we were planning to do.

"There's the studio lot," Aunt Peg said as she pulled the car over to the curb. "We're here early. The studio crew is probably still out to lunch. Are you positive you want to wait around until it's time for your audition appointment?"

"Yep," Mandy answered as she got out of the car and pulled her makeup kit and duffel bag out of the front seat. "I'll show Randi and Sandi around until it's time for my audition."

Randi and I got out of the back seat and shut the door behind us. "We'll see you after the audition, Mom," Mandy said.

"Good luck, honey," Aunt Peg said to Mandy. "Have fun, girls," she said to us. Mandy closed the car door, and Aunt Peg drove away.

"Well, now we're on our own," Mandy said. "I feel bad about pulling this stunt behind Mom's back. But I can't resist the chance to get even with Tara."

I could see that Randi was as nervous as I was about our little switcheroo plan. I wondered if we should really go through with it. "We could still change our minds about this you know," I said as Mandy picked up the bag.

Mandy paused. She looked me in the eye. "Do you want to?" she asked. "If you do, I won't mind, really. I'll understand."

"I don't want to chicken out," Randi fired back instantly.

Now the ball was in my court. "No, I don't want to change my mind, I don't think," I answered.

"That settles it," announced Randi. "Let's go knock 'em dead." And she started for the studio gate.

"Shall we?" I asked Mandy.

"Lead on," she replied. We marched off, following Randi.

At the gate the security guard checked our names off a list on his clipboard. She pointed out the building where the audition was to take place.

"I know the way, thank you," Mandy said as we started from the gate.

"Gee, they sure make you feel important around here," Randi said.

We walked past a lot of big buildings before we came to studio B-28. There we met another security guard.

Again the guard checked our names off a list. "Everyone is out to lunch," he told us. "But you can wait in the makeup trailer behind the stage until they come back." He opened the door for us and smiled as we walked past him.

When we got to the studio, all I could say was WOW! I'd never been in a studio before. The room was really huge. The stage area was in the center. It had fake trees, shrubs, and grass that looked real. The background was a beautiful painting of mountains and a cloudy sky. There were three cameras with cables that ran into a control room that was separate from the studio. People in the control room could look through a large glass window into the studio. Hanging from the high ceiling were lights of all shapes and sizes.

"It's pretty neat, huh?" Mandy commented. Randi and I nodded in agreement. "That's the makeup trailer over there," Mandy said. She pointed at a small trailer that was close to the stage but behind the camera area.

"Hey, we'll even be able to watch and hear each other from there," Randi said. "This will be even better than I thought."

"We'd better get in there before someone sees all three of us together," Mandy instructed.

"Right," I agreed. "They might put two and two together and come up with three look-alikes."

Randi and Mandy laughed at my little joke. We walked over to the trailer and went inside. The trailer was deserted when we entered it. It had small makeup rooms inside. We all crammed into one room and locked the door behind us. The room had a tiny glass window in the back. Through it you could see the stage area.

"Let's get ready for show time," Mandy said. She began to put on her makeup. Randi opened the duffel bag and took out more clothes just like what Mandy was wearing. Randi began to change. I removed my glasses, took my contact lenses out of the bag, and put them in my eyes. We dressed and put on makeup, and we all styled our hair the same way. When we were finished, we stood shoulder to shoulder and gazed into the dressing room mirror.

"Perfect," Randi said. "I can hardly tell us apart."

"They say you can't fool all the people all the time, but we will!" Mandy said. Then we heard people out in the stage area.

Mandy went over to the window in the back of the dressing room and peered through the glass.

"The crew is back from lunch," she announced. "There's Mr. Thorne, the director, and Mr. Butler, his assistant." Randi and I scrambled over to the tiny window. Mandy pointed them out to us. "It's almost time for me to get out there," she said. "Now, we've gone over everything that you have to do. Do you have any last minute questions?"

"Nope," said Randi.

I shook my head.

Mandy smiled. "Great! Well then...a star, I mean, three stars are born," she said.

"Go team!" shouted Randi, and then she put her hand over her mouth.

Just then, there was a knock at the locked dressing room door. It startled us so much that we almost jumped out of our skins. We must have sounded like a herd of trapped elephants.

"Mandy, are you all right?" a woman asked.

"I-I'm fine," Mandy called back as she fluffed her hair. She leaned close to us and whispered. "It's Mr. Thorne's script girl."

"Are you almost ready?" the woman asked. "The cameras will be up in about 10 minutes."

"I'll be right out!" Mandy called. We heard the woman walk out of the trailer.

"Okay, kids, it's show time!" Mandy announced. She winked at us and unlocked the door. "Remember the lines come first, then the jingle, and then the back flip. The cameras will stop rolling and give us time to switch places."

Randi and I gave her a thumbs-up. We had gone over all of that at least 10 times. "Break a leg," Randi said.

"We don't say that in TV," said Mandy. "They say it in theater. It means good luck."

"Oh," said Randi. "Well, then, break whatever you want."

Mandy laughed and went out. We locked the door and sneaked back over to the window to watch and listen. "This will be a cinch," Randi assured me. "Nothing can go wrong."

I crossed my fingers and hoped she was right.

Five

WE watched Mandy walk away from the trailer. Suddenly, she stopped. She turned to look at someone we couldn't see and made a sour face.

"I'm surprised you even bothered to show up," someone said. Then we saw who that someone was. A girl with curly, red hair and freckles strutted up to Mandy. It was Tara Butler. Randi and I booed softly like we did when Darth Vader came on the screen.

"I auditioned this morning," Tara continued. "Walter, that is Mr. Thorne, just loved my work. He thought my singing and my back flip were super," Tara bragged.

Mandy didn't say anything.

"I really have the part already," Tara continued. "He's just letting you audition to be polite."

"Who does that carrot head think she is?" Randi whispered to me. "I should go out there and slug her. Then she'd have a red nose to match her hair."

"Shhh," I said to Randi. "Mandy can handle Tinsel Town Tara. She's even nastier in person than I thought she'd be."

"If your audition was this morning," Mandy said to Tara, "why are you still hanging around?"

"For your information," Tara replied angrily, "Uncle Lyle took me out to lunch in the studio dining room."

Just then the script girl came up. "Are you ready, Mandy?" she asked. "Do you know your lines?"

"Yes," Mandy said to the script girl. "I'll see you later," she said to Tara and walked off.

The script girl took Mandy to the set.

"You're going to do a fine job for us, aren't you, Mandy?" Mr. Thorne asked Mandy in a loud voice.

"Yes, sir," Mandy answered.

Mr. Thorne told Mandy where to stand and gave her some directions. The camera angles were checked. A prop person gave Mandy some gum to chew. Mr. Thorne sat in his chair. A person with a shooting slate walked out in front of the cameras. He stood before Mandy and shouted, "Purple Power Bubble Gum Commercial—Mandy Daniels—take one!" and clicked the slate top down.

"Action!" shouted the director.

Mandy chewed the gum and smiled into the camera. "When I want a treat that's neat," Mandy began, "I reach for the top gum around. I chew Purple Power Bubble Gum—YUM!" Mandy finished by blowing a big purple bubble and letting it pop on her face.

"Cut! That was great!" Mr. Thorne shouted as he jumped up. "We don't need a second take.

Let's go right into singing the jingle."

"Um, Mr. Thorne?" Mandy called as she began to peel the splattered bubble gum off her face. "Can I have a second in the makeup room to get rid of this gum?"

"Okay, but make it quick," Mr. Thorne replied.

Mandy rushed toward the trailer. She passed Tara along the way.

"Not bad," we heard Tara say. "I can't wait to hear you sing. I need a laugh."

Mandy didn't stop to trade insults. She headed right for us. "Get ready, Sandi," Randi said to me. I nodded and went over to the door. I put my hand on the bolt. After I heard Mandy knock I pulled back the bolt, let her in, and relocked the door.

"Go, Sandi, go," Mandy said. "But be careful. Tara Butler is snooping around out there."

"I know. We saw and heard everything," I said.

"Good luck," Randi said as Mandy opened the door for me. "Break anything," my sister said. I took a deep breath and stepped out of the dressing room.

I was more than a little nervous as I walked out of the trailer, but I tried not to show it. *Just forget about all the people here, and pretend you're in your room singing to the radio,* I told myself.

"Well, the canary returns," Tara said as I passed her. I ignored her and went right in front of the cameras, still pretending I was all alone in my bedroom.

"We're all set," Mr. Thorne said to me. "Are you ready to sing the jingle, Mandy?"

"Yes, sir," I replied and smiled a big smile. *Whew,* I thought, *no one suspects a thing.*

"Don't worry about any music," Mr. Thorne went on. "We don't need it for an audition. Just sing the jingle when I cue you." I smiled again and nodded.

The cameras started to roll. The jingle part of the commercial was slated. "Action!" yelled the director.

I began to sing in my best voice. "Purple Power

is the one. It's a super bubble gum. If you're smart, you'll try some...Purple Power Bubble Gum!"

"Cut!" yelled Mr. Thorne. "That was terrific!" he shouted. "Mandy, you're a gem," he said.

"Thank you, sir," I replied after a short pause.

"Get ready for the back flip sequence," Mr. Butler, the assistant director, called.

"Uh, excuse me, sir," I said waving to the assistant director. "Could I be excused for a minute?"

"Why?" he asked.

"Ummm...I left something important in the dressing room, and I can't do my flip without it," I explained.

"Okay, but hurry up," Mr. Butler said.

I rushed off camera. "Where'd you learn to sing like that?" Tara demanded as I went by. "You could never sing before."

"Wait until you see me do a back flip," I replied as I hurried past her.

I dashed into the trailer and knocked on the dressing room door for Mandy to let me in.

"Now...don't break anything," I said to Randi as we traded places. Randi smiled and left. Mandy closed and locked the door. We went over to the window to watch. We got there just in time to see Randi stick her tongue out at Tara as she walked by. "That's just like Randi," Mandy whispered to me as Randi got ready to do her flip.

"Action!" yelled the director.

"Purple Power Bubble Gum will make you flip!" Randi shouted. Then she did the most beautiful back flip I've ever seen her do. She landed right on her feet facing the camera with a huge smile on her face.

"Cut!" the director yelled. He rushed up to Randi and put an arm around her shoulder. "Mandy," said Mr. Thorne, "that was terrific! I've seen all I need to see. The job is yours."

"Yippee!" Randi yelled. And she did another perfect back flip.

"Humph!" we heard Tara grunt loudly. We watched as she stormed off in a fit of anger.

Inside the trailer, Mandy and I gave each other

high fives. "It was a real team effort," Mandy said. "Did you see Tara's face? I'll never forget that look as long as I live."

"We sure taught her a lesson," I said. Then we remembered Randi and plastered our noses back against the window.

"The only thing to do now is to introduce you to the representative of the gum company," Mr. Thorne said to Randi. "He'll have the final say after he reviews this audition tape." Randi nodded. "I'm sure there will be no problem. He gave me the power to pick the girl lead for this commercial."

"The girl lead?" Randi asked.

"Yes," Mr. Thorne replied. "It's a big secret, but I can tell you now. You'll be doing this commercial with a famous boy actor. His name is Judd Morrison."

"Judd Morrison!" shouted Randi. She let loose a piercing squeal that almost shook the lights above. She ran howling all the way back to the trailer.

"I'll have someone call your parents to arrange the papers!" Mr. Thorne called after Randi. He was laughing.

Randi crashed into the trailer and pounded on the door. Mandy jerked it open, and Randi fell into the room.

"Did you hear? Judd Morrison," she sputtered. "Judd Morrison! I'm going to work with Judd Morrison!" she repeated over and over. I had to clamp my hand over her mouth to quiet her down.

"I'd better go out and talk to Mr. Thorne before he wonders what happened," Mandy said. I nodded. Mandy went out and closed the door behind her. I took my hand off of Randi's mouth.

"Now, be quiet, or you'll ruin everything. Somebody's going to hear you," I told her.

Randi looked bizarre. There was a goofy gleam in her eyes. "Judd Morrison," she whispered over and over again. Then she laughed and kept saying, "I'm going to work with Judd Morrison."

Six

RANDI finally started to snap out of it. She shook her head as if she still couldn't believe her good luck. "I'm going to meet tall, dark-haired, blue-eyed Judd Morrison. He's the hunk of the century. He's the star of *The Reckless and the Ambitious*. And I'm going to work with him," Randi cooed.

"Get real, Randi," I said. "Knock it off. You're not going to work with Judd Morrison. You're not going to meet Judd Morrison. You're not even going to *see* Judd Morrison!"

If looks could kill, the way Randi looked at me would have knocked me dead. "Sandi, what are you talking about?" she asked.

I took a deep breath. I hated to bring my sister back to the real world, but I had to do it. This Judd Morrison thing was getting out of control.

"Don't you remember our agreement?" I reminded her. "We only pretended to be Mandy long enough for her to get this job. Now Mandy will get sick, so Tara can have the part." I looked at Randi. She was in a state of shock. Her mouth was open, and her eyes were staring straight ahead. "That does ring a bell, doesn't it?" I asked.

"S-S-Sick?" Randi sputtered.

"That's right," I answered. "Mandy gets sick, and Tara gets the part."

"T-Tara gets our part," Randi grumbled. "Tara gets to work with Judd Morrison?" Randi gulped. "I'm the one who is going to get sick," Randi sighed. "I feel dizzy."

I went over and put my arm around my sister. "I know how you feel," I said, trying to comfort Randi. "But that was the deal."

"That's some deal," Randi mumbled. "This is a

once in a lifetime thing. There has to be some way I can get to meet Judd Morrison."

"There is!"

Randi and I turned to look behind us. Mandy was standing in the doorway. We had forgotten to lock the door after Mandy had gone out.

Mandy's words seemed to breathe new life into Randi. She jumped out of her chair and stared at Mandy. "What do you mean?" Randi asked anxiously.

Mandy closed the door, locked it, and began to explain in a low voice. "Mr. Thorne told me this commercial is very important to the Carter Candy Company," Mandy began. "It's the first one in a series of commercials that they plan to do."

"So?" urged Randi. She didn't care about the Carter Candy Company. She didn't care about Purple Power Bubble Gum. All she cared about at the moment was Judd Morrison, and that's what she wanted to hear about.

"So," continued Mandy, "Mr. Thorne wants

me, I mean us, to do a dress rehearsal with Judd Morrison for Mr. Carter, the owner of the Carter Candy Company."

"That means I can get to meet Judd Morrison!" Randi cried happily.

"Exactly," Mandy went on. "Since it'll be a rehearsal, it won't make any difference. I can pretend to get sick after the rehearsal."

"And I'll be able to meet Judd Morrison," Randi sighed. She had a really goofy look on her face.

"Hold on a minute," I said. "We're getting into deep water here. And I have this awful feeling in my stomach that we're going to end up in trouble."

"Maybe you're just hungry," Randi said. "I am. After all, we didn't have any lunch."

"I'm not hungry," I corrected. "Every time we start switching places, something goes wrong."

"What can go wrong?" Randi argued. "Nothing went wrong today. It was easy. It will be just as easy next time." She looked at Mandy. "Right?"

Mandy nodded. "Right," she agreed. "The commercial is going to be shot here. We can follow the exact same plan."

I shook my head. "It won't work twice," I said. "I just know it won't. Something will happen."

"Sandi, you always expect the worst," Randi said. "You agreed to help when Mandy needed you. Now I need your help to meet Judd." Randi folded her arms across her chest and frowned.

"Well, suppose Aunt Peg and Uncle Nick find out," I said. "Mom and Dad will be out here next week. Suppose they find out. I don't want to end up grounded until my 18th birthday."

"My sister, the worry wart," Randi muttered.

I glared at Randi. "You'll risk anything to meet that soap opera airhead," I said. I started to change back into my own clothes.

"Yes, I would," Randi said slowly. "This is very important to me."

I looked at her and saw that her lower lip was trembling and that her eyes were red. That did it. How could I still refuse. "Okay," I said slowly,

"I'll go one more round."

Randi ran over and hugged me. "Thanks, sis. I knew you wouldn't let me down," she said. She was really happy. It made me feel good.

"You'd better hurry up and change," I said to Randi. "Aunt Peg will be waiting."

Mandy smiled at me. "Everything will work out fine," she assured me. "The rehearsal is a couple of days away. Mr. Thorne told me to wear a purple T-shirt and purple jeans for the rehearsal. I know a place where we can all get the same outfit."

"Well, I like the sound of that," I replied. After all, purple is one of my favorite colors. At least I'd get a new outfit out of this.

Mandy went over to the window to check the studio. Most of the crew had already left. The ones who remained were busy. They'd never notice us leaving. "Are you ready to go?" Mandy asked.

Randi buttoned her jeans and nodded. I nodded, too. "Well, let's scram," Mandy said as she picked up her bag. "I'll go first and make sure the coast is clear." Mandy unlocked the door. She went out and checked around the trailer. She came back in a few minutes. "Let's go," she urged. We sneaked out of the dressing room and out of the trailer. Then we scooted through the dark studio toward the exit. No one saw us. We walked out past the building guard. He smiled at us.

"Wait until Mom hears I got the part and beat out Tara," Mandy said as we headed for the main gate. "She'll really flip."

"Hold on a minute," chuckled Randi. "Flipping is my department, remember?" We all laughed as we left the lot and walked toward Aunt Peg's car, which was parked at the curb.

Seven

"I still can't believe you beat out Tara Butler for that Purple Power Bubble Gum spot," Aunt Peg said, frying bacon for breakfast the next day. "That role is really demanding with the singing and back flip and all. I almost fell over when Mr. Thorne called to tell me the news."

Uncle Nick put down the morning paper he was reading. "What's even more amazing," he said, "is that you beat out Tara when her uncle is an assistant director for the commercial." He sipped his coffee.

"How did you ever do it?" Aunt Peg asked Mandy.

Mandy shrugged her shoulders. "It was just

luck, I guess," she replied.

"Well, whatever it was, Mandy," Uncle Nick said from behind the newspaper, "you sure proved you're no dreeb."

"Uh, I think you mean dweeb, Dad," said Mandy rolling her eyes at us.

Randi stopped munching on her buttered toast. "Luck nothing," Randi said. "It was pure talent. You should have seen that back flip. Wow! It was awesome!"

I glared at my sister across the table. She made a silly face and went back to munching on her toast.

Aunt Peg put a platter of bacon, eggs, and home fries on the table. "I didn't even know you could do a back flip," Aunt Peg said to Mandy. "When did you learn to do that?"

Mandy gulped and served herself a little breakfast. I noticed she didn't take very much. "Oh, Randi showed me how to do it," Mandy said. "With Randi's help, doing a back flip was easy." Mandy passed the platter to Randi.

Randi dug right into the platter. She piled about three pounds of breakfast onto her plate and then passed it to me. I served myself and sent the platter on its way around the table.

"So, what do you girls have planned for today?" Uncle Nick asked.

"We're going shopping," Mandy replied. "We have, I mean, I have to get a purple outfit for the commercial."

"Speaking of the commercial again, Mandy," Aunt Pet began. "Isn't that young actor, Judd Morrison, supposed to work with you?"

Randi almost choked on her breakfast. "Are you all right, Randi?" Uncle Nick asked as he got to his feet.

Randi gulped down some orange juice. "I-I'm fine," she replied. "I guess I ate too fast."

"Right, you ate too fast," I said.

Uncle Nick wiped his mouth with his napkin. He picked up his jacket and briefcase. "I've got to get to work," he announced. "Can I drop you girls at the mall on the way?"

Mandy put down the peach she was nibbling on. "That would be great," she said. "But then Mom would get stuck doing the dishes."

"Oh, I don't mind, this time," Aunt Peg replied. "Go ahead."

"Thanks," we all said and got up. Randi was still coughing.

After getting our things, we went outside and got into the car. Mandy, Randi, and I all piled into the back seat.

"I feel like a chauffeur," Uncle Nick said.

"Beautiful movie stars always have handsome, young chauffeurs, Uncle Nick," I said.

Uncle Nick let us off at a corner near the mall, and we walked across the parking lot. The mall was beautiful. I was looking forward to spending a relaxing day just browsing.

"Wow, this is really something," Randi muttered as we walked inside the huge glass and chrome doors.

"There are three shopping levels," Mandy explained as she led us toward the escalators.

"There are tons of great stores and a neat boutique on the bottom level that has some really rad fashions," she said. "We'll get our outfits and spend the rest of the morning hanging around and window shopping."

"That sounds great," I said. We rode the escalator to the bottom level and walked to the boutique. It was a totally awesome place. All the mannequins were made of shiny metal. The sales clerks looked like fashion models from Mars. We sure had nothing like that back home.

We began to look around. The store wasn't crowded at that hour in the morning.

"These purple jeans would be perfect," Mandy said as we stopped near a pants rack.

"And those T-shirts would match," Randi said as she pointed at another nearby rack.

We all picked out identical jeans and tops. "Let's go try them on," Mandy suggested. "The fitting rooms are over there." She pointed to the other side of the store.

"You two go ahead," I said to Randi and

Mandy. "I'll be there in a second. I want to look at those pink skirts."

"Okay," Randi replied as she and Mandy headed for the dressing rooms. I began to look at the skirts that had caught my eye. Mandy and Randi weren't gone long before I heard a voice behind me.

"If you're looking for a monkey suit, you're in the wrong store."

I turned around and came face to face with Tinsel Town Tara. I was caught completely off guard. I didn't know exactly what to say or do. I just crossed my fingers and hoped Mandy and Randi would take their time in the fitting room. Was I ever glad I'd worn my contacts instead of my glasses. There was no way Tara could tell I wasn't Mandy.

"H-Hello, Tara," I said, trying to be polite and friendly. "How are you?"

"I'm out of a job, thanks to you," Tara grumbled.

I shrugged my shoulders. "That's show biz," I

replied. "You can't win 'em all."

Tara looked at me in a funny way, like she was studying my face.

"You look different," she mumbled. "I don't know exactly what it is, but you don't look like the Mandy Daniels I know."

"Maybe you don't know the real me," I said. I fidgeted a bit and sneaked a peek at the dressing rooms. The coast was clear, but I was nervous.

"Your hair is different," Tara said.

"It's parted differently," I answered.

"But it's not just the looks," Tara continued. "It's something about your mannerisms." I shrugged as if I didn't know what she was talking about. "Most of all it's that singing you did at the audition. I know for a fact that you can't carry a tune in a basket. You have a singing voice like a hoarse chicken."

Tara was starting to make me mad. Why couldn't she just accept that she couldn't win all the jobs. You win some. You lose some. I knew that from soccer. She acted like she had a right to be in all the commercials.

"Did you have a voice transplant or something?" she asked with a mean look on her face.

That did it. I know it would have been better to just ignore her. But I said, "You ought to think about getting a personality transplant, Tara." And I walked off toward the fitting rooms. I hoped Tara wouldn't follow me.

"Oh, yeah!" she shouted after me. "There's something weird going on. And I'm going to find out what it is!"

Tara picked up her packages and stormed out of the boutique. I stopped near the fitting room curtains and watched her leave. As soon as she was gone, Mandy and Randi poked their heads through the curtains.

"Whew!" Randi whistled. "That was close. It's a good thing we heard her and stayed in the fitting room."

"Well, there goes our shopping spree," I said. "With Tara prowling around the mall, we'd better head for home as soon as I try on my clothes."

We all squeezed into the fitting room. "This switcheroo is starting to have some definite drawbacks," I complained.

"But look at all the advantages," Randi argued as I tried on my purple jeans.

"Name one," I said.

"Well, I get to meet Judd Morrison," Randi answered.

"Don't say that name to me. I'm sick of hearing his name," I said. I couldn't wait until that rehearsal was over. I couldn't get rid of the feeling that something bad was going to happen.

"Okay, you guys. Let's pay for our clothes and get out of here," Mandy urged. "That Tara is such a snoop that she might just come back."

Eight

I was so nervous the day of the big rehearsal that I hardly said a word during the ride to the studio. Randi was the exact opposite. She was so excited that she chattered nonstop every bit of the way. Of course, all she talked about was Judd Morrison.

"It sounds like Randi kind of likes Judd Morrison," Aunt Peg joked.

"Kind of?" I asked. "That's an understatement."

"Well, today she'll finally get to meet him," Mandy said.

"That's right," Aunt Peg said to Mandy. "Make sure you introduce him to your cousins."

"Oh, I'm sure he'll meet Randi," Mandy said.

I felt bad for Mandy. I could tell by the way Mandy looked that she felt bad about fooling her mom. But what else could we do? It had already gone too far. Besides, if we chickened out now, Randi would die of a broken heart.

"Are you sure you want to get to the studio so early again?" Aunt Peg asked. "You're way ahead of schedule."

"That's because Randi wants a chance to talk with Judd Morrison before they start shooting," I broke in. I felt awful about lying to Aunt Peg, but what I said was partly the truth.

"I still think I should stay for the rehearsal," Aunt Peg said as she pulled the car over near the studio gate.

"No, mother! Please don't!" Mandy cried as she placed a hand on Aunt Peg's shoulder.

Aunt Peg parked the car and shut off the engine. She looked at Mandy who was beside her in the front seat and then glanced back at Randi and me. "Girls," she began, "you're all acting a little strange. Is there something going on?"

"No, Mom," Mandy stated. "It's just that if you sat in now...well, it would be bad luck. After all, I got this callback without you being there."

Aunt Peg looked at Mandy. "Well, all right," she said. "But this is the last time I'm going to allow you to go alone. Besides, Randi and Sandi's parents and little brother will be here before the final taping of the commercial. I'm sure they'll want to see you perform."

Mandy gulped and nodded.

That's one commercial Mom and Dad will never see, I thought to myself. I didn't even want to think about Terrible Teddy on the loose in a movie studio. Instead of a commercial, it would end up as a disaster flick. I was glad this would be our last trip to the studio.

"We'd better get going," Mandy said. Mandy collected her makeup kit and bag. We got out of the car.

"Girls," Aunt Peg said, leaning out the window. "Are you sure there's nothing going on?"

"What could be going on?" Mandy asked. "Mom, you've been watching too many mystery shows on TV."

"Well, maybe," Aunt Peg said. "Good luck, honey. I'll see you later." She started the car and pulled away.

When she was gone, Mandy breathed a sigh of relief. "That was close," she said. "Mom suspects something. Luckily, after today this will be all over."

"I could say I told you something like this would happen," I said as we walked toward the gate. "I could, but I won't."

"You just did," Randi said as the guard checked our names and passed us through. At Studio 28-B, the guard at the door greeted us.

"Good morning, ladies. You're here early," the guard said.

"We like to be on time," Mandy replied. We went right into the studio with Mandy leading the way. Some technicians were working on the set, but no one else was around. It was safe. We walked into the makeup trailer.

"We should have no problems," Mandy said as we went into the dressing room we'd used before. "Judd Morrison will use a regular dressing room in the building. No one will come in here except us."

"Great," I said as we squeezed into the small room with the tiny window. Mandy placed the duffel bag on the couch in the corner. She opened it and took out the three sets of purple jeans and T-shirts. She hung them up in the small closet near the couch. Then she opened her makeup kit.

"We'd better start dressing right now," Mandy instructed. Randi and I nodded. We put on our makeup and dressed in our purple outfits. Time passed quickly. Out in the studio, lights went on, and people began to arrive.

"Let's get our hair done," I suggested.

"Good idea," Mandy agreed. We crowded around the one mirror in the dressing room and started to style our hair to look exactly the same.

We were elbow to elbow.

"This is too cramped," I complained. "Since no one is going to come in here, I'm going into one of the other dressing rooms and use the mirror in there."

"Smart thinking, Sandi," Randi complimented. "I'll use another dressing room, too. I want to look extra good today."

"I wonder why?" I teased.

"Okay," Mandy said. "But be careful."

I unlocked the dressing room door, and peeked out. "It's okay," I said to my sister. Randi and I crossed the narrow hall area to the other dressing rooms. I went into the room directly across from the one Mandy was in. The dressing room was a carbon copy of the one I had just left. The only difference was that its tiny window looked out on the other side of the trailer behind the studio area.

I started to fix my hair so we would all have the same style. Now that I finally had some room, it didn't take long. When I was finished, I got up

74

and went out into the hall. Before I could reopen the door to the dressing room Mandy was in, the main door to the trailer opened. Into the sitting area stepped the very last person I wanted to see. You guessed it—Tinsel Town Tara!

"Well, surprise! Surprise! If it isn't Mandy Daniels," she said.

"Well if it isn't...Tara Butler!" I said very loudly so Randi and Mandy would hear me. "What are you doing here...Tara?" I practically screamed the sentence.

"Why are you yelling?" Tara asked.

"Yelling? I'm not yelling...Tara!" I said at the top of my lungs.

"And why do you keep repeating my name?"

"You mean your name...Tara!" I bellowed.

"You're getting weird, girl," Tara said. I stood in the middle of the passageway so she couldn't come any further.

"So what are you doing here?" I repeated. I hoped that by now Mandy and Randi had gotten the message to stay hidden.

"Uncle Lyle brought me to the studio," she explained, "to meet Judd Morrison. He's some hunk. And, plus, he might be able to help my career."

I could have sworn I'd heard Randi growl. I wondered if Tara heard her. "Good for you," I said in a snippy way. "Now what do you want in here?"

"Mr. Thorne sent me in to see if you're almost ready," Tara said. "He wants to talk to you before Judd arrives."

"Tell him I'll be right out," I answered.

Tara didn't leave. She just stood there, staring at me. "You changed your hair again," she said. "It was different at the mall."

"So what? I wear it different ways for different days," I answered and waved my hand.

Tara came closer. She looked me square in the eye. "Something's going on here," she said. "Something's just not right." She gave me a dirty look. "I know for a fact you can't sing a note. But you sounded like Barbara Streisand the other

76

day. How did you do that?" she sputtered as she threw up her arms in confusion. "If I didn't know better, I'd swear you had a ventriloquist help you!" Tara turned around and stomped out of the trailer.

"It's safe to come out now," I called to Randi and Mandy. The doors to their dressing rooms opened. They popped their heads out.

"Say, where is that ventriloquist?" Randi joked as we squeezed back into Mandy's dressing room. We all laughed. And the more we thought about Tara and how puzzled she was, the more we laughed.

Nine

"WELL, I'd better get out there," Mandy said as she finally stopped giggling.

I nodded. I forced myself to stop laughing and peeked out the window toward the studio area. "There are a lot of people out there," I said.

"Is Judd Morrison there?" Randy asked as she jumped up on the chair beside me. She covered her eyes with her hands. "I can't bear to look!" she cried.

"You can look. He's not there," I replied.

"You'd better lock the door after I go out," Mandy instructed.

"I'll do it," Randi replied.

"Good luck!" I called from the window.

"Thanks," Mandy answered as she went out. Randi closed and locked the door. Then she joined me at the window. We watched Mandy walk over to Mr. Thorne and Mr. Butler. We didn't see Tara. The script girl was near Mr. Thorne. There was another man there, too. He was kind of chubby and bald.

"Hey! That guy looks familiar," Randi said to me.

"I know," I said. "I recognize him from somewhere, too. But I can't place him." Then it struck me who he was. "He's the guy from the plane and the airport!" I told Randi. "Remember?"

"Yeah," Randi said. "I wonder what he's doing here?"

"Be quiet, and maybe we'll find out," I said.

"Hello, Mandy," greeted Mr. Thorne. "I asked you to come out here early so you could meet Mr. Howard." The bald man reached out to shake hands with Mandy.

"Hello, Mr. Howard," said Mandy.

"Mr. Howard is from the Carter Candy

Company," Mr. Thorne explained. Mandy and Mr. Howard shook hands. He looked at Mandy very closely.

"Have we met before?" Mr. Howard asked.

Mandy shook her head. "No, sir," she replied. "I don't think so."

"It doesn't matter," Mr. Howard continued. "I liked your work on the tape. You look like an honest and trustworthy person. That's the kind of person we want for our commercials."

Mandy gulped. "Th-Thank you, sir," she answered.

Mr. Thorne smiled at Mandy. "We'll get started as soon as Judd arrives," Mr. Thorne said. He turned and looked toward the entrance to the studio. "Here he comes now."

"Look!" squealed Randi. "EEEK! It's him! It's really him. It's Judd Morrison! Catch me, Sandi. I'm going to faint."

"Shhh," I said. I turned back to the window. I didn't think Judd Morrison looked as tall or as handsome in person as he did in his photos.

In fact, he looked kind of ordinary to me.

But he didn't act ordinary. He acted as if he were someone real special. Following Judd were a skinny man in a baggy suit, a well-dressed lady with a notebook, and a man in a chauffeur's uniform.

"Judd, it's good to see you," Mr. Thorne said and held out his hand. Judd didn't bother to shake hands with Mr. Thorne.

"Right," Judd answered, looking around the studio with a bored look on his face.

I could see that Mr. Thorne felt awkward. He slowly dropped his arm to his side. "This is Mr. Howard, from the Carter Candy Company," Mr. Thorne introduced. "And this is Lyle Butler, my assistant director." Judd didn't bother to shake hands with them either. He just nodded at them.

"This is a real honor," Mr. Butler said. "My niece, Tara, is dying to meet you." He looked from side to side. "Now where did she go? She's around here somewhere."

"Don't bother to hunt for her," Judd said. "I

don't have time to meet every kid who has a crush on me. I want to get this rehearsal over with. I've got things to do and people to meet." He looked at the three people behind him. "Right?" he confirmed.

"Right, Mr. Morrison," answered the man in the baggy suit.

"Right, Mr. Morrison," answered the woman with the notebook.

"By the way," said Judd, "let me introduce my agent, my private secretary, and my chauffeur and bodyguard. Please get them some refreshments. Now, can we get to work? My time is valuable."

"Work?" asked Mr. Thorne. "Oh, yeah. By the way, I forgot to introduce a very important person." He turned to look at Mandy. "This is Mandy Daniels, the girl you'll be working with."

"Hi," Mandy said as she stepped forward.

Judd didn't say hello. He just said, "Before we start, Mandy, let me give you a little advice." He put his arm on Mandy's shoulder.

"What advice?" Mandy inquired.

"Don't fall in love with me, kid," he teased. "I'll only break your heart." And he burst into laughter. Then the man in the baggy suit, the woman with the notebook, and the chauffeur all laughed, too.

"I'll try real hard not to," said Mandy.

"Okay, folks, everything is ready," Mr. Butler announced. A prop girl gave Judd and Mandy some Purple Power Bubble Gum to chew. Mr. Carter sat down just behind the cameras. Mr. Thorne began to talk to Mandy and Judd Morrison.

"Judd is a conceited snob," I said to my sister. "He's just a jerky Hollywood wise guy. He's a semi-regular on a crummy soap opera, and he acts like he's already won an Oscar!"

Randi smiled her goofy smile at me. "He's wonderful," she sighed.

"Didn't you hear him?" I asked.

Randi shook her head. "I think my heart was pounding too loudly to hear anything," she replied. "But he looks great. I just wish I could see him better."

"Humph!" I grunted as I got down from the window. "Why don't you go outside for a better look at your hero?"

"Hey! That's a great idea," Randi replied. She got down from the window and walked toward the door.

I jumped up. "Randi! You can't!" I shouted. "Someone'll see you." I blocked Randi's path. "It's too risky."

"No one will see me," Randi answered. "I'll hide behind the trailer. They'll all be too busy rehearsing the first part of the commercial. I'll just watch for a minute and then sneak back in here."

"No," I pleaded.

"Yes," Randi said.

"NO!"

"YES!"

"No."

"Yes. Now, step out of the way, Sandi. I have

to do what I have to do."

There was no way I could stop her. "Be careful, at least," I whispered.

Randi opened the dressing room door. I watched her go to the trailer's exit. She opened the exit door a crack and peeked out. The coast must have been clear, because she slipped out and shut the door behind her. I closed the dressing room door and went back to the window. Mandy and Judd were just starting to rehearse.

"When I want a treat that's neat," Mandy began, "I reach for the top gum around. I chew Purple Power Bubble Gum. YUM!" She blew a big bubble.

"And that's the truth," said Judd as he looked into the camera and flashed his perfect rows of pearly white teeth. Then he popped Mandy's bubble with his finger.

"Great," said Mr. Thorne. He looked at Mr. Howard.

"I like it," Mr. Howard admitted.

"Good work," Mr. Butler announced. "But

let's go through it again."

Mandy got a new piece of gum. They went through the same bit several times. I watched but couldn't enjoy it. I was too tense. I kept thinking about Randi hiding somewhere out there. I wished that she'd come back already.

Before I knew it, Mandy's part of the rehearsal was over. "Let's move on to the jingle," Mr. Thorne announced.

"I'll be right back," Mandy said.

"Hey, where are you going?" Judd Morrison asked. "I want to get this over with." He looked at his watch.

"And I want to clean this sticky gum off my face," Mandy answered as she walked toward the trailer.

"Go ahead, Mandy," Mr. Thorne said before Judd could say another word.

Mandy came into the trailer and closed the door behind her. I was waiting in the hall. Mandy knew something was wrong from the look on my face.

"What is it?" Mandy asked. "Why are you out here?"

"It's Randi," I explained. "She went out to get a better look at Judd, and she hasn't come back yet."

"Oh, no!" Mandy groaned. "Couldn't she wait? Where'd she go?"

"She said she was going behind the trailer," I said.

"We'd better see if we can spot her before you go out," Mandy replied.

I nodded. We dashed into the dressing room on the other side of the trailer. We climbed up on a chair and looked out the tiny window.

"There she is," Mandy pointed out. Randi was hiding behind some big empty cardboard boxes that were stacked near the trailer.

"And that's why she hasn't come back," I explained. Mandy looked where I pointed. Standing in the background was Tara Butler. She had a clear view of the boxes and the studio area. If Randi got up, Tara would see her.

"She's trapped!" I said. "Now what?"

"Uh-oh! Now there's big trouble," Mandy groaned. I looked in the opposite direction. Judd Morrison was being led toward Tara by Mr. Butler. They were headed right past Randi. They were sure to see her.

"Tara!" called Mr. Butler. "So, there you are. Come over here, and meet Judd Morrison." Mr. Butler and Judd stopped right in front of Randi.

"Hey! What are you doing there?" Judd asked Randi. "I thought you went into the trailer. Quit fooling around and wasting my time." He stormed over to Randi, grabbed her by the arm, and yanked her out from behind the boxes.

"I...I...I..." Randi sputtered.

"Let's get back to work," Judd said. He started to pull Randi into camera range. "Let's do this jingle and get it over with."

"But what about meeting my niece?" Mr. Butler called after Judd. Tara was now at her uncle's side.

"Later," Judd answered as he dragged Randi

before Mr. Thorne. "Maybe."

"Sorry, Tara," Mr. Butler said. Tara looked mad enough to explode. Mr. Butler left her there to simmer and raced after Judd and Randi.

"Now we're in for it," I said to Mandy. "Randi will never be able to sing that jingle. I knew something like this would happen."

"We're dead," Mandy admitted. We hopped down and crossed the hall to the other dressing room. We closed the door and locked it. We jumped up on the chair and watched from the window.

Randi was standing under the lights in front of the camera. Did she ever look nervous.

"Are you ready to sing?" Mr. Thorne asked.

"I am," Judd answered as he took his place near Randi.

"I'm not," Randi gasped.

"Huh?" sputtered a surprised Mr. Thorne. "Why not?"

"Uh...Uh...laryngitis!" croaked Randi as she grabbed her throat with both hands.

"Laryngitis? In the summertime? In L.A.?" Mr. Butler asked.

Randi shrugged her shoulders.

"That was quick thinking," I said to Mandy. I crossed my fingers and hoped for the best.

"Let's try it, anyway," Mr. Thorne urged. They slated the part. "Action!" Mr. Thorne yelled.

Oh, no, I thought. *This is the end!*

"Purple Power is the one," Randi and Judd sang. "It's a super bubble gum. If you're smart, you'll try some...Purple Power Bubble Gum!"

Judd's voice was good, not great. Randi's voice was really awful. People on the set gritted their teeth as she sang. She not only made herself sound bad, but she made Judd sound bad, too.

"CUT! CUT! CUT!" hollered Mr. Thorne.

"That's not good," Mr. Howard said to Mr. Butler.

"It's laryngitis," Randi croaked again pointing at her throat.

"She was great at the audition," Mr. Thorne said to Mr. Howard.

"You're right. She sounded fine on tape," answered Mr. Howard.

"Fine!" screamed Judd. "This kid is flatter than a tomato run over by a cement truck. She stinks! I'm not used to working with amateurs." The man in the baggy suit ran up to Judd and gave him a glass of water. The chauffeur brought a chair.

"Hey!" Randi said to Judd. "Just who do you think you are, Mr. Big Shot? I told you, I'm sick. My throat hurts!"

Mr. Howard burst out laughing. I guess he thought Judd was a little obnoxious, too. Even Mr. Thorne smiled.

I was surprised to hear Randi speak to Judd like that. I guess she finally saw him for what he really was—a stuck-up creep.

"I'm sure Mandy will do better when her laryngitis clears up," Mr. Howard chuckled. "Let's go on to the back flip."

"Right," Randi said as she smiled from ear to ear. "Laryngitis hasn't affected my back flip."

"Okay, it's the back flip!" Mr. Butler shouted.

Judd Morrison glared at Randi as the cameras were readied for the next shot. "Don't mess this up, frog voice," Judd said.

Randi gave him a dirty look.

"Action!" Mr. Thorne yelled.

Judd smiled his big, phony smile for the cameras. "Purple Power Bubble Gum will make you flip!" Judd and Randi shouted. Then Randi did a perfect back flip.

"Cut! That was very nice!" Mr. Thorne called.

"I think I've seen enough," Mr. Howard said as he got up. "Let's go ahead with the taping as planned."

He walked over to Randi and shook her hand. "Nice job, Mandy," he told her. "I especially liked your dialogue with Judd." He laughed and walked away.

"That's all for today!" Mr. Butler called.

"Good work, Mandy," Mr. Thorne said to Randi. "Great work, Judd," he said.

Judd stared at Randi. Randi made a funny face

and stuck out her tongue at him. Then she walked toward us in the trailer.

"Judd," Mr. Butler called. He ran up to Judd and put an arm around his shoulders. "Before you go, you've got to meet my niece, Tara."

"Sure," said Judd, "why not?"

Ten

WE heard Randi stomp into the trailer. We opened the door, and she stormed into the dressing room. Mandy shut the door behind her.

"What a creep! I can't believe I ever thought he was cute. What a snob!" she said as she flopped down on a chair. "I'm never watching his nerdy soap opera again. Am I ever glad we don't have to work with him anymore."

Randi's face was all red. I'd never seen her so steamed up. She folded her arms and gritted her teeth. Her eyes were all watery. I thought she was going to cry. I felt so bad for her that I almost cried myself. First she has this crush on the guy, and then she finds out how awful he really is. I went over and put my arm around Randi. Mandy came over, and we just sat there together for a while.

"Randi," I began. "Let's make a deal. I'll never mention his name again, if you promise me just one thing."

"What thing?" Randi asked.

"Promise not to sing anymore! You're awful!" I cried.

I started to giggle, and then Mandy did, too. Randi smiled a little bit and then started to laugh, too. When we finally stopped laughing, Randi asked, "Was I really that bad?"

Mandy didn't answer. She just held her nose with her fingers. "But your flip was outstanding," she added.

"Outstanding," I repeated.

"Let's get out of here," Randi said. "I've had enough show biz for one day." She smiled and got up.

"Hold your horses," I cautioned pushing her back into her chair. "We've got to wait for everyone to leave. We don't want a Hollywood rumor to spread that Mandy Daniels is triplets."

"Right," Mandy agreed. "That would be it for my career. Besides, it shouldn't be a long wait. They'll break for lunch any time now."

* * * * *

After what seemed like a long time, Randi whined, "How much longer do we have to wait? I'm starving."

"What else is new?" I asked. "Actually, I'm a little hungry myself," I admitted.

Mandy climbed up on the chair and looked through the window. "Okay," she said. "I think everyone's gone. Let's go."

We grabbed our stuff and went out of the dressing room. We sneaked out of the trailer and headed for the door. "We're home free now," Randi whispered to me. "See, Sandi, I told you there was nothing to worry about."

"Ah-ha! I knew it!" came a shout from the

shadows. We froze dead in our tracks. Then we slowly turned around.

Tara stepped out from behind the cardboard boxes Randi had hidden behind earlier. "Now, what do we have here?" she asked. She folded her arms across her chest and walked up to us. "There are three stooges instead of one."

Mandy gulped. "Okay, Tara. You're right," she said. "These are my cousins, Randi and Sandi. They're identical twins who are visiting me during summer vacation."

Tara checked us out one by one. She shook her head in amazement. "I knew you couldn't sing, Mandy," she said. "Which one of these two did the singing?" She pointed at Randi. "Was it Tweedle Dee?" Then she pointed at me. "Or, was it Tweedle Dum?"

"You better watch it, Tinsel Town," Randi muttered.

"Take it easy, Randi," I said as I stepped forward. "I did the singing," I told Tara. "I'm Sandi. My sister, Randi, did the back flip," I explained.

101

"Well, well, is that so?" Tara asked. She gave Mandy a dirty look. "I knew if I hung around long enough, I'd find out what a sneaky cheater you are."

I could tell Randi was really getting mad at Tara. Randi has one of the worst tempers around when she gets riled up. "Mandy wouldn't have had to cheat if she had an Uncle Lyle to get jobs for her."

Tara shot Randi a nasty look, but Randi added, "Or, if Mommy and Daddy could have hired gymnastics and singing coaches."

"Look, Tara," said Mandy, trying to be nice, "We didn't mean to be sneaky or cheat. It was supposed to be just a joke...on you." Mandy sighed. "But it backfired."

"It sure did," Tara scoffed.

"I'm sorry, really," Mandy said. "We weren't going to finish the commercial. We, I mean, I planned to get sick and drop out before the taping, so you'd end up with the part."

"Oh, sure you were!" Tara mocked. "I'm *really*

supposed to believe that?"

"It's the truth!" I shouted. "We would have dropped out right after the audition except that Randi wanted to meet Judd Morrison."

"I think you're all liars," said Tara.

"What are you going to do?" Mandy asked Tara.

"I'm going to tell Uncle Lyle everything," Tara said. "And when he tells Mr. Thorne about the trick you played on him, you'll be finished. You'll never make another commercial as long as you live." Tara turned and walked off.

Mandy's chin dropped to her chest. She looked really worried. "Now what?" Randi asked.

"First, we'd better get out of here. Aunt Peg's waiting," I said.

"Tara's right," Mandy moaned as we walked out past the guard at the exit. "I'll never work again."

"Don't worry, Mandy," I said. "We'll think of something."

"I'm ruined!" Mandy cried.

"Stop it, Mandy," I said firmly. "We've got a few days before the taping. We'll come up with a plan."

As we passed through the main gate, we saw Aunt Peg waiting for us. "Who ever thought a vacation in Hollywood could be so much trouble?" I asked as we walked to the car.

Eleven

THE next day, Mandy kept pacing back and forth in her room. "Tomorrow is doomsday," she moaned. "The commercial shoot, Tara, Judd Morrison..."

"Yep, tomorrow is doomsday in more ways than one," agreed Randi. "Mom, Dad, and Teddy are arriving tomorrow for their vacation."

"By tomorrow night, I'll be a Hollywood has-been, and we'll all be grounded for life," Mandy said as she started back across the floor.

Randi sat up. "Maybe what we need is a plan," she suggested.

Mandy stopped pacing. She glared at Randi. I did, too. "No more plans," I said. "I think it's time to tell the truth about everything."

"I agree," Mandy said. "What choice do we have? Besides, I'd like to get this off my chest. This worrying is killing me." She flopped down in a chair. "I know Tara must have squealed. What I don't understand is why Mr. Thorne hasn't called Mom yet."

Randi shook her head. She got up and picked up pacing where Mandy had left off. "It sure is strange," Randi admitted. "Everything's going on like nothing happened. I guess they just expect us to show up for the commercial."

"I don't understand it at all," I said. "Unless, nobody believes Tara."

"Hey!" said Mandy as she jumped to her feet. "You know, maybe you're right. Maybe they think she made it all up."

Randi had a sly smile on her face. "Now if that's so, we could just have Mandy show up alone for the taping," Randi began. "She could stink at the jingle and flip, and that would solve everything. No one would ever know what we did except Tara. And who'd believe her?"

"*I'd* know what we did," I said quietly. "It wouldn't be right."

"I'd know, too," Mandy agreed.

Randi looked at Mandy. Then she glanced at me. "I guess you're both right," she agreed. "It's time for the truth. We better start by telling Aunt Peg and Uncle Nick the whole story."

"Okay," Mandy agreed with a sigh. "The Three Musketeers will bravely face the firing squad together," she uttered. "But we might as well wait until tomorrow morning to break the news."

"That's a good idea," I said. "That way we won't have to repeat the gory details for our mom and dad when they get here. We can tell everybody our tale of woe at the same time."

Randi sighed loudly. "Okay, but let's wait until after breakfast to spill the beans," she said. "If I'm going to die, I want to at least die with a full stomach." We all laughed. But it was a nervous kind of laughter.

* * * * *

"Staying home to make breakfast while Mom and Dad pick up your folks and Teddy was a good idea," Mandy said.

I nodded at her as I lifted some pancakes off of the griddle. I stacked them on a platter near some others. Randi buttered the new stack.

"This is going to be some breakfast," I said as I looked at the table we'd set. We'd made pancakes, eggs, home fries, sausage, toast, coffee, and anything else we could think of. It was a welcoming feast for Mom, Dad and Teddy. Randi said that it was also a good way of buttering up the judges before they listened to our case.

"They're here!" Mandy announced as she glanced out the kitchen window into the driveway. I suddenly felt so excited that I forgot all about the trouble we were in. We tore off our aprons and rushed out the back door.

The first thing we saw was Teddy. He hopped out of the car and ran toward us.

"Ranee! Sanee! Manee!" he cried as he waved his arms.

"Hi, Trouble!" I shouted as I bent down and gave him a big hug and an even bigger kiss.

"Hi, Mom! Hi, Dad! Welcome to Hollywood," Randi called as my parents came up the sidewalk.

"Hi, girls," Mom answered.

We all took turns hugging and kissing everybody else.

"Is all the mushy stuff over with now?" joked Uncle Nick as he piled suitcases on the kitchen floor.

"I think so," I answered.

"Hey! Something sure smells good," Aunt Peg said.

"I hungree!" Teddy yelled. He raced over to the kitchen table and climbed up on the chair at the head of the table. We all laughed.

"I guess it's time to eat," Uncle Nick said. "It looks great."

I walked over to my brother, and the rest of the

family sat down. "What do you want, Teddy?" I asked. "Pancakes? Eggs? Toast?"

"I want Yum-Yum-Yummy Super Pops!" Teddy answered at the top of his lungs. "Super Pops with moze." Moze was Teddy's baby word for milk.

"We don't have Super Pops," Randi said to Teddy. "Have some eggs."

"Eggs yuckie!" Teddy shrieked. "Yum-Yum-Yummy for your tummy, Super Pops!" Teddy continued.

"He loves that cereal," Mom explained to Aunt Peg and Uncle Nick. "And he loves the commercial."

"What a coincidence," Aunt Peg said. "The girl in that commercial is named Tara Butler. She's the one Mandy beat out for the commercial you're going to see this afternoon." Aunt Peg got up and went to the cupboard. She took out a box of Super Pops cereal and fixed a bowl for Teddy.

Mom and Dad looked at Mandy. "We can't

wait to see you perform, Mandy," Mom said.

"Yeah," Dad agreed. "I bet you're totally radial."

"That's radical, Dad," Randi said. She lifted a fork stuffed with pancakes to her mouth and began to nibble.

"Right. Totally radical," Dad corrected.

Mandy took a big drink of orange juice and looked at me. "Well, I guess it's now or never," Mandy said.

"Good-bye, hearty breakfast," Randi groaned as she put her fork on the table.

"Yum-Yum-Yummy Super Pops!" Teddy sang as he spooned cereal into his mouth.

"Mom, Dad, Aunt Peg, and Uncle Nick," I began. "We have a confession to make."

"It's about that commercial and how I got the part," Mandy added.

"Uh-oh, I knew something was going on," Aunt Peg said.

"Let's hear the confession," Uncle Nick urged, setting down his coffee cup.

We began to explain what had happened. We took turns telling what we did and why we did it. Everyone listened carefully. Even Teddy didn't interrupt. He was too busy wolfing down his Super Pops cereal.

"Tara said she was going to tell her uncle, and that's the last we heard about it," Mandy concluded at last.

Dad looked at Uncle Nick. Mom looked at Aunt Peg. "Girls," Dad said finally, "switching identities always backfires on you. What you did this time was as wrong as last time. You should have known it wasn't going to turn out okay." Dad tried to look stern. But he didn't sound very mad.

"We know that, Dad," Randi said. "But that Tara is so obnoxious. We did it to help Mandy, and to teach Tara a lesson."

"Tara is unbearable," Aunt Peg admitted. "But that's no excuse."

"What I want to know," Mom cut in, "is what are you going to do now? It sounds to me like

Mandy's career and reputation are in real danger."

I looked at Mom. "We talked it over," I began, "and we decided to go to the studio this afternoon and face the music."

"That's right," Mandy agreed. "We're going to tell Mr. Thorne and Mr. Howard the whole story. But we'll leave out the part about how awful Tara is."

Uncle Nick picked up his cup of coffee and sipped it. Then he nodded. "I don't approve of what you've done," he said. Then he smiled and added, "I can't believe you pulled it off. It really was a great plan."

"We'll all go to the studio together," Aunt Peg said. "Letting you go to the studio alone helped contribute to this mess in the first place."

"Yum-Yum-Yummy for your tummy, Super Pops!" Teddy yelled as he finished the last spoonful of cereal. "Dat was dood."

Twelve

AT the main gate to the studio, the guard checked our names before allowing us to pass. Together the Daniels family must have looked like some group. It was lucky that Aunt Peg had cleared our visit with the studio's security department way in advance.

"The Daniels family—a party of eight. Go ahead," the guard said.

This is not going to be a party, I thought as we walked toward Studio 28-B. The guard at the studio smiled at us and held the door open.

"Dat policeman was nice," Teddy said as Dad carried him into the studio. "Where's his gun?"

"He's not a policeman, Teddy," I whispered to

my little brother. "He's a security guard."

"But," Teddy said, "he has policeman badge." It's useless to argue with Teddy, so I just let the subject drop.

"So, this is what a real studio looks like," Mom said as we walked toward the makeup trailer.

"It sure is something," Dad said as he looked around at all the lights and wires.

Standing in a group near the stage area were Mr. Thorne, Mr. Howard, and Mr. Butler. They had their backs to us as we approached. Off to one side was Judd Morrison with his three assistants. Near him was Tara Butler. The rest of the crew was busy. It was Tara who spotted us first.

"There they are!" Tara yelled as she pointed at us. "I told you there were three of them. See! I didn't make it up."

Judd Morrison looked over to our group. When he saw the three of us, his mouth dropped open in amazement.

Slowly, Mr. Thorne, Mr. Howard, and Mr. Butler turned to face us. They stared at us in silence as we approached their group.

Uncle Nick and Aunt Peg stopped. Mom and Dad halted, too. "Go ahead, girls," urged Uncle Nick as he gave Mandy a nudge forward. "This is your show. We'll wait here."

"I go, too," Teddy said as he tried to wiggle out of Dad's arms like a puppy.

"No, Teddy," Mom said quieting him. "You stay here."

Led by Mandy, Randi and I walked toward Mr. Thorne and Mr. Howard. Mr. Butler crossed his arms and frowned at us. "I knew Tara wouldn't lie," he remarked to the other two men. "Today they're dressed differently, and their hair styles are different. But it's easy to see that they tricked us. They're as alike as three peas in a pod."

Mr. Thorne glanced over at Mr. Butler. "Can it, Lyle!" he ordered. We stood in front of Mr. Thorne and Mr. Howard.

"Now I know where I saw you before!" Mr. Howard cried. "You were those funny twins on the plane," he said laughing.

"Yes, sir," I admitted. "I'm Sandi Daniels. This is my twin sister, Randi."

"Randi and Sandi Daniels?" Mr. Thorne mumbled, scratching his head.

"They're my cousins, Mr. Thorne," Mandy explained. "My dad is the brother of their dad and my mom is the sister of their mom. That's why we look so much alike."

"Make them tell you how they fooled you to get this part!" Tara cried as she came rushing over. "It was a trick. Mandy Daniels can't sing or do a back flip. They cheated! I should have gotten that part."

"You're right, Peg," I heard Mom whisper behind us. "That child is a bit too much."

Mandy spoke up. "Tara's right, Mr. Thorne," Mandy admitted. "Sandi did the singing. Randi did the back flip. And I read the lines."

"Wait a minute. Wait a minute," said Mr. Thorne, shaking his head. "I can understand how you two could stand in for Mandy. You look so

much alike that it's astonishing. But how did you trade places at the audition and the rehearsal without us noticing?" he asked.

Mandy explained about dressing the same and how we'd used the trailer to swap places. She told them everything. She finished by admitting we were wrong to do what we'd done. Then she apologized to everyone including Tara and Judd Morrison.

"Well, I guess that means the part is mine now," Tara snapped.

"You mean I have to work with Freckles over there," Judd Morrison groaned as he joined our group. "What is this, a commercial or musical chairs?"

"Be quiet, both of you," Mr. Thorne commanded. "The decision is up to Mr. Howard." Mr. Thorne looked at Mr. Howard who was standing quietly, listening to everything.

Mr. Howard looked at Randi and Mandy and me for a while. Then he burst out laughing. "This is the funniest story I've ever heard," he chuckled. He made himself look serious. "However, it was wrong to trick us like that, girls," he continued. "And since honesty is what we're looking for in this commercial, I think Tara gets the Purple Power Bubble Gum part."

Tara smiled at her uncle. Mr. Butler smiled back at Tara.

"Can we get to work now?" Judd asked. "I've got better things to do than to stand around wasting time. Nancy," he called to his assistant, "what time is Robert Redford's reception?"

"It's at 8:00, Mr. Morrison," she answered.

"Set up for the opening shot," Mr. Thorne called to the crew.

Mr. Howard looked at us. "Sorry about this, girls," he apologized.

"That's all right," I answered.

"I guess we deserve what happened," Randi said.

"That's show biz," said Mandy glumly. We turned and started to walk back to our folks.

Thirteen

"**N**ICELY done, girls," Uncle Nick said when we rejoined the group.

"I'm proud of you, Mandy," Aunt Peg said as she hugged Mandy. "That wasn't an easy thing to do. I know how badly you wanted to beat out Tara for that part."

"I'll beat her out next time," Mandy vowed.

"You sure will," I said.

"I hungee," Teddy called as he squirmed in Dad's arms.

"Did you hear that?" Dad asked. "It must be feeding time again for the Daniels herd. Let's go get a snack. The treat's on me."

We all turned and started toward the exit. We

didn't get far before we heard Mr. Howard calling to us.

"Just a minute!" he shouted as he walked up to us. "I was just thinking about something," he said. "When that little boy said he was hungry, it reminded me of it."

"That little boy is our brother, Teddy," I told Mr. Howard. Then I introduced him to the rest of my family including Uncle Nick and Aunt Peg.

"Teddy reminded me of another commercial we're going to be doing in the near future," Mr. Howard explained. "It's for Triple Treat Candy Bars. It starts with a little boy telling his sister he's hungry—just like Teddy did."

"Really?" Mom replied.

"Yes," continued Mr. Howard. "But I was just thinking...instead of one sister, the boy could have three sisters. Get it? Triple Treat, three sisters. And it would be great if the sisters were identical."

"You mean..." sputtered Mandy.

"Yeah!" cried Mr. Howard as he nodded. "You

three girls would be perfect. Are you interested?"

"Are we interested? You bet we are!" Mandy exclaimed.

"Yes sir!" Randi cried.

"We're interested, for sure!" I added.

"All I need now is a little boy to smear chocolate all over the girls' faces," Mr. Howard said. "That's the concept we have in mind."

"I hungee!" Teddy shrieked.

Mr. Howard looked at Teddy. Then he looked at us and smiled.

"Teddy?" I asked as I pointed at my brother.

"Why not?" asked Mr. Howard.

Teddy grinned. "Yum-Yum-Yummy, Super Pops!" he hollered. "I hungee. I want Super Pops!"

"Change that to Triple Treat Candy Bars, and we've got a deal," Mr. Howard said chuckling.

"It's a deal," Teddy said as he shook hands with Mr. Howard.

"A star is born," I said. And everybody laughed.

About the Author

MICHAEL J. PELLOWSKI was born January 24, 1949, in New Brunswick, New Jersey. He is a graduate of Rutgers, the State University of New Jersey, and has a degree in education. Before turning to writing he was a professional football player and then a high school teacher.

He is married to Judith Snyder Pellowski, his former high school sweetheart. They have four children, Morgan, Matthew, Melanie, and Martin. They also have two cats, Carrot and Spot and a German Shepherd dog named Spike.

Michael is the author of more than seventy-five books for children. He is also the host and producer of two local TV shows seen on cable TV in his home state. His children's comedy show, "Fun Stop," was nominated as one of the best local cable TV children's shows in America.